Butterfly Books
PUBLISHING

See You Later, Alligator

Written by Alicia Kelley
Illustrated by Novel Varius Rizal Apriaji
Edited by Rob B Daniel

Hardcover ISBN: 978-1-7360444-0-7
Paperback ISBN: 978-1-7360444-1-4

See You Later, Alligator

Written by
Alicia Kelley

Illustrated by
Novel Varius Rizal Apriaji

Dedicated to and inspired by my grandma,
Bernice Armstrong.

I love and miss you.

I can't wait, today's going to be a great day.
I'm going to my grandma's house to play.

Saying goodbye is the hardest of all,
And if my grandma wasn't so silly, I'd probably bawl.

My name is Billy
But my grandma's so silly!

Sometimes she doesn't call me that...

One time she said, **"See you later, Alligator!"**
What? An alligator?

I don't have scaly skin.
I don't like to swim.

I have a short little nose,
And Mommy makes me wear clothes.

And my belly won't touch the ground,
Unless I'm playing around.

But then I get dirty and see Mommy's wrath,
And the worst thing of all, I must take a bubble bath.

And I'm pretty sure alligators don't take bubble baths.

Silly grandma,

I'm definitely not an alligator.

Another time she called,

"Toodleloo, Kangaroo!"

What? A kangaroo too?

Well, I do like to jump, just not all day long.
And on my little body, those big feet don't belong.

I don't have pointy ears,
And if I did there'd be tears.

I can't hold a baby in my belly,
And I only eat peanut butter and jelly.

And I'm pretty sure kangaroos don't know how to make peanut butter and jelly.

Silly grandma, I'm not an alligator,

and I'm definitely not a kangaroo.

And sometimes she says,

"See you next time, Porcupine."

What? A porcupine?

No way! I'm not even pokey - that's your first sign.
And I only eat leaves, from time to time.

I'm not nocturnal, I sleep all night long.
Well okay, that's a little bit wrong.

Shhhhh, can you keep a secret?
So Mommy doesn't fret,

Instead of sleeping,
I'm usually sweeping.

Okay, not really. I usually just play with my legos.

And I'm pretty sure porcupines don't even have legos.

Silly Grandma, I'm not an alligator,
I'm not a kangaroo.

And I'm definitely not a porcupine!

Oh! And one time she said, **"Farewell, Gazelle!"**
What? A gazelle?

I don't have horns coming out of my head,
And I don't believe grass makes a great bed.

I am the fastest in my class,
But I'm not quite as fast

As a gazelle being chased by a big scary cat.
But I can outrun my neighbor's cat.

His name is Paul.
But he is rather fat, and not fast at all.

So, I am pretty sure a gazelle would not be that scared of Paul at all.

Silly Grandma, I'm not an alligator.
I'm not a kangaroo.
I'm not a porcupine.

And I'm definitely not a gazelle.

And that time she said, **"Bye-bye, Butterfly!"**
What? A butterfly?

Although I would like to, I can't really fly.
And I've never been able to reach up to the sky.

I'm also quite big
And too heavy for twigs.

And I don't have wings.
But if I did I'd decorate them better,
Drawing tractors and trains and all those boy things.

But I still might get cold during a Michigan storm,
My grandma knits me sweaters, that's how I stay warm.

And I'm pretty sure butterflies don't have grandmas to knit them sweaters.

Silly Grandma, I'm not an alligator.
I'm not a kangaroo.
I'm not a porcupine.
I'm not a gazelle.

And I'm definitely not a butterfly.

One time she even said, **"Take care, Polar Bear!"**
What? A polar bear?

I don't have fur and I'm not quite that pale.
The snow makes me go, "brrrr," and I don't have a tail.

Oh, but if I did, all the things I could do.
I could use it as a brush to paint my sister's face blue.

Wag it around and tickle her senseless,
But nonetheless,

I **don't** have a tail.
And I'm pretty sure polar bears don't have sisters they want to put for sale.

Silly Grandma, I'm not an alligator.
I'm not a kangaroo.
I'm not a porcupine.
I'm not a gazelle.
I'm not a butterfly.

And I'm definitely not a polar bear.

The next time she said, **"See you soon, Baboon!"**
Really, a baboon?

Sometimes Mommy says I act like one,
But I know I don't look like one.

They like to scream,
And I only scream for ice cream.

I walk on two legs
And can make scrambled eggs.

And I am pretty sure baboons cannot make scrambled eggs.

Silly Grandma, I'm not an alligator.
I'm not a kangaroo.
I'm not a porcupine.
I'm not a gazelle.
I'm not a butterfly.
I'm not a polar bear.

And I'm definitely not a baboon.

There was one time she said,

"Hit the trail, tiny snail."

Okay, I am tiny, but not that tiny.
I am also not in the least bit slimy.

Okay, I'm pretty sure I don't have to explain this one!

Silly Grandma, I'm not an alligator.
I'm not a kangaroo.
I'm not a porcupine.
I'm not a gazelle.
I'm not a butterfly.
I'm not a polar bear.
I'm not a baboon.

And I'm definitely not a snail!

But today was different, because Grandma said something different.

For her goodbyes she looked in my eyes, and said,

"Goodbye Billy, I love you!"

'Billy,' that's me, and will always be me.
And I will always be me, as me as can be.
And I'm not quite sure, but I am pretty sure,

That me being me is why my grandma loves me.

Printed in Great Britain
by Amazon

11752206R00016